Praise for Amina Cain's CREATURE

"To be among Amina Cain's creatures is to stand in the presence of what is mysterious, expansive, and alive. Whether these distinctly female characters are falling in and out of uncanny intimacies, speaking from the hidden realms of the unconscious, seeking self-knowledge, or becoming visible in all their candor and strangeness, they move through a universe shaped by the gravitational pull of elusive yet resilient forces—the yin-dark energies of instinct and feeling that animate creative life. It's here that the intuitive reach of fiction meets the reader's own quest for understanding, through the subtle beauty of living the truth of one's experiences in the most attentive and unadorned way possible." PAMELA LU

"Amina Cain is a beautiful writer. Like the girl in the rear view mirror in your backseat, quiet, looking out the window half smiling, then not, then glancing at you, curious to her. That is how her thoughts and words make me feel, like clouds hanging with jets, and knowing love is pure." THURSTON MOORE

D1557798

First Edition
ISBN: 978-0-9844693-8-3

Art on cover © 2013 by Catherine Lemblé
All rights reserved

Design and composition by Danielle Dutton
Printed on permanent, durable, acid-free recycled paper
in the United States of America

Dorothy, a publishing project
St. Louis, MO
dorothyproject.com

CREATURE
AMINA CAIN

To Amar
and to Lucien

"Drink, my angel; everything I have inside me is yours, soak it up through the paper, through the sleeve of my coat. Suck my blood out of the hollow of my elbow where you are lying, where you are keeping warm. It's just as you please, it will always be just as you please from now on." VIOLETTE LEDUC

A THREADLESS WAY

When I first moved here, I lived in a friend's room in a loft. I had never lived in a loft before, and it was strange to do so in such a quiet place. Downtown was unlike any downtown I had ever been in: its emptiness surprised me, but it was empty only of certain kinds of people. They were around, but they lived on the sidewalk and in tents. And stores and businesses existed, but not the kind tourists want to shop at. The month—August—was hot, the way I like weather to be, and in the evenings when it cooled down I rode my bike through the neighborhoods next to mine, and sometimes to a cornfield that someone had planted nearby. I would get off my bike and look at the plants, at the cobs of corn hidden in their pale green husks. I liked that the field was there, with the city's buildings so close to it. I liked that I was there.

Across the street from where I lived was a school of architecture, and the huge, dusty lot in front of the long building comforted me like the cornfield did. The building had once been a train station, and the friend whose room I was subletting had gone to this school. Even with all this comfort, though, I felt like a weird person. Sometimes in the loft I could barely hold my head up as I talked to people.

I couldn't look them in the eyes. I was happy, and settled in my new life, but I was also limp, and maybe still shell shocked by the anxiety I had regularly felt before moving. The people who lived in the loft had been there for a while, and I was an outsider who had come to stay in the empty room.

In the living room area, several aloe plants sat on a table in front of large windows overlooking the school, and a motorcycle was parked in the corner. There were also several desks scattered around. Once in a while I sat at one of the desks to write, but mostly I worked in my bed.

One night a guy who lived in a tent several blocks away from the loft said to me, "You don't look like a confident person." Was my lack of confidence apparent to people on the street? I didn't feel limp when I was alone, when I was walking around the city. I felt good then.

Summer extended itself into September and its sun was harsh and healing; evenings were extremely pleasurable. It's said you can't run away from your problems, and I knew that was true—I still had some problems, but others had completely disappeared. Some part of life was closed to me, but another part was open. I had nothing to do really, except go to yoga classes and the grocery store. Those things usually took a whole afternoon or evening, so in doing them I felt I had been out around the city, had accomplished something. And I liked doing them. The yoga studio was small and clean; and in the bathroom, instead of disposable paper towels, neatly folded washcloths were set out on a shelf. I had already lived an adult life in my old city; why was I now living a life so different from the one before?

In the loft the walls didn't reach the ceiling, so I was never alone. One of my housemates also studied architecture at the school across the street, the way my friend had, but did most of her work from home. Her room was right next to mine and I could hear her move around, even in her bed. Our other housemate left in the mornings and returned at night. When he was at home, he worked on drawings at one of the desks while wearing headphones. He also ate there, and watched things on his computer.

Sometimes I talked on the phone, knowing my housemates could hear what I said. I talked about a project I was helping to organize in my old city, and I talked about how life was going for me in the new one. I wanted to advertise to my housemates that I had lived in a place where I had had a job, and also still had responsibilities, even if I had none where I was now living.

During that time, I saw a movie about a woman who lived out of her car with her dog because she didn't have any money, and then lost the dog while traveling through Oregon. When she lost her dog, I couldn't stop crying. I've always felt a lot for animals, but I also related to the woman who lived out of her car. I thought I might be like her.

One day I drove to the middle of nowhere with my friend whose room I was living in. He was home on a visit from Dubai. Once we had been very close, but those days were gone. Still, we attempted to spend time together.

The sun was unimaginably harsh; I drove while my friend slept in the car. When he woke up we stopped and got out to climb some rock formations that looked like they were crumbling, even though they were stuck to each other. Together the rocks formed a micro-climate for plants that grew in the shade they made, and for animals who could also survive there, because of the shade. Short trees had sprouted up, and delicate plants. Little squirrel-mouse animals scurried around, though they weren't quite squirrels, or mice. We sat under the shade of one of the trees to watch them. We didn't let our arms or our legs touch.

At night the air turned from hot to warm and then it got chilly.

"We don't know each other," I said.

"Yes, we do."

"We're more like brother and sister now."

When we went down in elevation on the ride home it got warm again. There was no water around, but I felt it, like we were descending into a large, shallow sea.

At home, I crawled into bed and read a story I had read many times before, that I had taught in some of my classes. There was something in that story I wanted to sink into: the rich darkness of a barn, the putting the hand out into that darkness to see what it touched. I was no longer close to one friend, but I was becoming close to another. I thought about this second friend while pulling the covers over me. I lay all the way down, covering my head and face. You are a writer, I thought. "Dante!" someone yelled somewhere outside the building. Four flights up in the middle of a desolate downtown, that is where you are. I closed my eyes, but I didn't sleep. Instead I saw the darkness, and then rock formations running into that darkness.

What I didn't understand was how my friend and I could have become distant when we were probably more interesting people than we had been when we were close; though I was weaker than I had been when we were close, and he was stronger. This probably had something to do with it. When I thought of the second friend I felt comforted. The first time I felt this was when I had stopped by to visit him and he was asleep. I knocked on his screen door and he woke up to let me in. He wore a *churidar* and a pink shirt that was starting to tear on one of the shoulders. He got back into bed and I sat in his desk chair next to him and we talked about a book he was reading.

I continued to wander around the city, absorbing something from it. I had very little money, but I've always identified with not having much, so it didn't bother me, except when I couldn't afford to make credit card payments. One evening I rode my bike through a neighborhood where cheap clothes were sold. I bought myself a dress for $9.99. It was pretty—turquoise with small black polka dots all over it, and sleeves that rose stiffly from my shoulders. I wore it to a museum, where in one of the galleries I saw four ornate wooden chairs facing a whipping post. Lights shone on the chairs and on the post where the wood had splintered and turned old. On a gleaming table sat a pair of slave shackles surrounded by intricately carved silver vases. An artist had found these things in a historical society in Maryland and exhibited them there together. Now they were here. I touched my dress, its cheap material.

"What do you want from this city?" my friend had asked me in the car on our way home.

"Nothing. Just to live in it."

"That's not true."

"It is true." With no traffic on the freeway my friend drove fast, much more so than I would have. "What do you want from Dubai?"

"I want what everyone wants."

I looked at him and saw that he had a scratch on his face. "Which is what?" I asked.

He never answered.

When I left the museum it was starting to rain, and a guy called me over to his tent. It was a simple triangle, like the one my parents and I had taken camping when I was young.

"What?" I asked him.

He shrugged. "I'd like to invite you in."

"Why?"

"You seem like a nice woman."

"I am."

"Your arm bends in a weird way," he said.

I held my arms up in the rain. "I know, it always has. Both of them."

"Are you going to come in?"

"No."

"Your loss." He unzipped the tent door and bent down to crawl inside. I could see part of a blue sleeping bag and a few magazines stacked on top of it. A lantern hung from the middle of the ceiling and the guy turned it on. "Have a good night," he said.

"You too."

Back at the loft I stood looking out of the window, at the school, its long shape extending into the darkness, at my arms, my shoulders in my dress. I made it look like my arm was as long as the school.

Later, when I had lived here for a while, my second friend and I visited an orchid estate. It was finally cold outside, but the greenhouse was warm. Water droplets collected on the plastic covering and window panes. I walked around looking at the orchids, at their ways of being in air. Some of them seemed like they were holding it, like they were spoons or bowls; some faced the air, slender prongs pointing up, slender fangs pointing down; some pushed through or away, small, strong flaps with light yellow ridges or dark red spots. I looked at the plants for a long time. Then I sat down in a chair and wrote in my notebook. I noticed it become evening. When I finally saw my friend again, he was carrying two orchids.

In the car, we situated the plants in the back seat so they wouldn't fall over, and rolled the windows down so they would get some circulation.

"Can we drive by the university?" I asked. "I'd like to see what the campus looks like."

"Sure."

We drove through the campus where the lights from the buildings shone out onto the grass. The buildings were new with hardly anything to distinguish them from each other, except that some of them had more floors than the others, and in front of the library was a sculpture that looked like a coat hanger. A few students were sitting on it. I tried to imagine myself teaching there.

"That's enough," I said. "I just wanted to have an idea so I could picture it in my head."

It felt like something weird was going to happen, but nothing happened. I turned around and looked into the backseat. The orchids were upright; everything was the same. I thought back to the period of time when it had taken me half an hour to eat a piece of toast.

Back then it had seemed as if I was living a life after it had already ended. Now I could hardly take in enough.

ATTACHED TO A SELF

Sometimes there is a great emptiness, like shaking a box nothing is inside of; sometimes the box becomes warm. It was like that when I arrived here. It was four in the morning and before coming I had been reading a book about being an adult. I had also been trying to read *The Flower Ornament Scripture.*

I can't picture you doing that.

It's not weird, is it?

I guess not.

I don't know yet what I'm walking around in. I feel lost. I like that. A sentence in the introduction to *The Flower Ornament Scripture* reads, "It could variously be said with a measure of truth in each case that these teachings are set forth in a system, in a plurality of systems, and without a system." So there is a web, but that web doesn't actually exist, and sometimes it is multiple.

Do you think you are walking around in a web?

On the way here, the person I was driving with asked me lots of questions about my life. I asked her lots of questions too, and though I thought I could go on for a long time in that way, I wanted to respect the silence of the place we were going to, so I watched what I could see of the ocean, then what I could see of the hills, their lumpy shapes above us, and then again at the line of the ocean running alongside.

On my first night, before the bell was struck to begin evening zazen, there were many sounds I had never heard before and they came through my head and my heart at strange angles.

Often, in my first weeks here, I would wake up from a nap, something piercing through me. There were many things moving through my mind and they seemed to combine into a single arrow.

I settled in.

One of my favorite times here, when I most feel a part of the community, is when we carry things together. Twice a week someone from the monastery goes into town to buy the things we need for the coming days, then comes back, usually during dinner. We have to stop eating to carry vegetables from the truck to the walk-in or to the pantry. I love everyone then. I also like when there are talks at night in the dining room, because it's a chance to be with the others in a different way, in chairs, waiting for someone to begin speaking. I look around at people talking and laughing at a time when we are usually silent. I've never lived in community before.

Do you think it's reality?

Yes, it's real.

I've started a reading journal. I don't have very much time for books, but I sit down with one whenever I can. Behind the zendo is a library. Behind that is where we wash our clothes. Sometimes when I'm reading I can hear the water come on and off, splash into the plastic buckets or the sinks. The library is very small; if four people are in it, it's crowded. If it's just you and one other person it's intimate, like you had planned to read together. Once, when I got to the library, my driving companion was there, reading a book. We smiled at each other and I climbed the ladder to the reading loft.

What kinds of things do you write in your reading journal?

Yesterday I copied down: "Is the body a religious practice?" Do you think that's silly?

What did you do today?

I sat and thought about a thing in so many different ways that I was able to turn it in various directions and look at it. This might be obsession, but if it is, it is a new kind of obsession, a new way for me of being obsessed with something.

That sounds vague. What were you thinking about?

It's kind of boring. I thought about whether or not I am the kind of person who should live in a monastery.

In *The Diamond Sutra* it says, "However many beings there are in whatever realms of being might exist, whether they are born from an egg or born from a womb, born from the water or born from the air, whether they have form or no form, whether they have perception or no perception or neither perception nor no perception, in whatever conceivable realm of being one might conceive of beings, in the realm of complete nirvana I shall liberate them all. And though I thus liberate countless beings, not a single being is liberated."

When I come across a sentence like that I usually get very excited, but lately this sutra has been frustrating for me. I am studying it, but it is disruptive. Every few days I meet with three other people and we read and discuss the sutra. Sometimes we chant it. We have been trying to find new ways to approach it, but it's been difficult. For some reason, even though I enjoy the new ways, they make me laugh and I am afraid this laughter is disturbing the others. I don't want to bring down our study. I laugh when we chant; the others sound so serious, and so nice. It's as if we are throwing ourselves at the sutra; I feel, specifically, that I am throwing myself against a wall of it, though I am never injured, only come to know how flat and hard it is.

This evening after dinner I hiked up past the solar panels with one of my friends. It's more of a climb than a hike, actually. On part of the trail is a rope so you can pull yourself up and also keep track of where you're going; the trail starts to disappear. My friend was wearing sandals and I think it was hard for him, harder even when we were coming down. There are small prickly buds on the ends of the dry grass that get stuck on my clothes whenever I hike here. They got stuck to my socks and dug into my legs. Every time we sat down for a rest I tried to remove some of them, but I always collected more. I thought I could sense the ocean by the color of the sky, but my friend told me I was looking in the wrong direction. It still seems as though the ocean is in that direction.

On the way down, we became covered in dirt and had to go to the bathhouse. There, the lanterns shone softly. I hardly ever go when it's dark out and I could barely see the other women around me, could barely see myself, when, after bathing, I combed my hair in front of the mirror.

I like picturing that.

Really?

Yes.

Do you feel distant from me?

Yes, I do.

The densho is calling me to evening zazen. Now someone is hitting the han. I love the han, the way the mallet sounds as it strikes the wood. The path is dark and someone is wearing a headlamp.

I'm sorry.

Why?

That we're distant.

If we stop talking to each other, I'll have to find a different way to communicate with you.

Will it really be me, if I'm not there?

I'm not sure, but I don't know what else to do. Sometimes I feel close to you when you aren't there.

In the zendo, we sit. Someone clears her throat, and the person next to me carefully changes his position. My shoulder blades are tense and I want to relax them. They are usually like that when I sit zazen. Outside, I can hear a person walking across the gravel, and even farther away, a person in the dining room, talking.

The land in this place is reminiscent of the desert. I think I needed everything that grows here. I'm happy, and I don't know what to think about that. I know there isn't a goal to find happiness, and yet I find it, even when things are hard. I don't really want to leave.

What do you think will happen then?

That I'll go back to being anxious.

Isn't that part of what you are doing there, to be okay with whatever is happening?

Yes. What's it like where you are?

It's hard. Someone I love is sick.

A few weeks ago, a visiting Benedictine monk who was giving a talk in the dining room spoke for a few minutes about reading. I might get this wrong, but I think I remember him saying that in his tradition the word is supposed to send a person into the great silence. Just a little bit of reading is enough. When I read I usually want to do so for a long time, but to read a little and then to be with that reading in silence sounds very nice.

Something about him reminded me of you, or what you might be like when you are older; I think the ways you both move around in your bodies.

I WILL FORCE THIS

Lately I've been having a hard time knowing what's good. I don't even know how to write. Maybe I am only a reader. I try to force things, force stories. I have to work on a story for many, many months before it makes sense.

Still, someone gave me the opportunity to copy a piece of writing onto the wall of a gallery. I'd never done anything like that before. I called it a hunger text, because it was about a woman who didn't have enough money for food. On the day I painted my hunger text on the wall, I wore an old-fashioned lace shirt that had once belonged to my aunt. I also wore a long wool skirt. The text was projected onto the wall, and I painted on top of it. I found it both relaxing and exhausting to do this all day.

I will write about this experience, I thought. Now I am writing about it, but I'm not sure what there is to say, and whether or not saying it will be interesting for anyone to hear or read. I felt comfortable painting the text while wearing the old-fashioned shirt and the skirt. I wanted to make a costume for myself, even though I wear this costume at other moments too, like when I go to the grocery store, or to a restaurant. Maybe I wanted to be another kind of writer, one who performs putting her text on a wall, as if it would be fun for someone else to see me do this.

Now she is painting an "A" on the wall, and now an "e." Now I have painted the word "foot." And now "pleasure." The woman in the text is projected onto the wall too, limping across letters, eating bugs. Can you see her? What am I doing there, leaning across her, leaning across those letters, while standing on a ladder, with the text projected on my back, and my arms, as my shirt is white, and see-through, and when I am there the woman is on my back and arms as much as she is on the wall.

Here, I have put a hungry, abject woman on the wall for you to ponder; a woman who still feels pleasure. If you read part of this text, you'll only know a little about her. If you read all of this text, you'll still only know a little about her.

I walked across the floor of the gallery, dragging my foot. No one else was in the room; this part of the performance was only for me. This must have been more interesting than seeing me paint letters on a wall. Watching me paint letters would only be interesting for someone who has some special attraction to me. I suppose if I were attracted to a person I could watch him or her paint letters on a wall all day, or at least for a part of an afternoon. I am in a relationship, but I am sure the person I am in a relationship with would be bored by having to watch me paint letters on a wall for more than ten minutes. This is understandable. But it felt good, the dragging of the foot. I liked doing it.

When I got home, my partner was eating an egg. This is what he does when I'm not around. He also eats fish. I was harsh to him, but without speaking. I expressed myself through the violent putting away of a pan. Later I sat on his lap and dreamed about the future. This was together alone.

In our reveries, we both forgot the other was there. I was very far away. I was thinking about how dark it was getting outside, but I clung to his neck, which must have meant that I was also very much in the room. When I told him what I had been thinking about, he didn't believe me. "How could you look so far away and be thinking about something so mundane?"

"But darkness is never mundane."

"I need to work now," he said gently, nudging me off his lap.

I wanted to wash my face and my feet. I wanted to be invited somewhere.

"This is evil," I said out loud.

The days went by and I occupied myself with reading and writing and lying around on the porch. In my mind I was very close to the days before when I had written my hunger text on a wall. Every moment felt charged with a thing that had just happened, or a thing that would happen once something else had ended. Lying around on a porch sounds lazy, but it doesn't have to be. It depends on how you feel about it. Because my wrists hurt, I was still charged with the copying of my piece of literature.

Finally I did start to feel lazy, so I walked a few miles along a surprisingly empty road to a university library, though I have no affiliation.

I collected the books I wanted to read, and then found a comfortable place to sit, so I could read them. This place happened to be next to an elevator, but that's not what made it comfortable.

"I want to see myself here," I said out loud.

The woman in the chair next to me jerked her head around. "This is a library," she said incredulously.

"I know. That's why I said it."

"Look in a window. At your reflection."

"I don't do that anymore."

"Study your arm."

"You don't understand what I'm talking about."

The woman stared at a row of books for a few minutes. They were hardbacks. Then she got up to watch a documentary about a writer. I could see the screen, but I couldn't hear anything. The woman was wearing headphones.

I will force this into a story. I got cold when I thought this. I started shivering. I was in a place where I couldn't control the temperature, which upset me. I wanted to be comfortable so I could focus.

I moved into a sunnier part of the library and continued reading. Right away I was able to see the specter of the story. Now I am moving through literature, I thought. I would like to move through something abject. Like when you touch something warm and you get warmer. But, I am abject myself. I don't need to touch another to feel this way. I possess it inside, like a little clamshell.

I was tempted to move in a way that would make the others in the library think of me strangely, the way I had moved when I was in the gallery.

I looked at my hand. How can I re-imagine you?

This can not be a portrait. The page is the size of a mirror, but that doesn't mean anything. Once I looked at my arm and wanted to write about that. Write about the arm when the whole body is being abused.

Tonight, the night I am writing this, I am sick and tender. My body is warm and it hurts my throat to swallow.

Not knowing what is good for anyone, I start writing.

I want to make another costume for myself. I want to perform another thing on a wall, like truth, but I don't know what truth looks like—I haven't experienced it yet.

I remember a moment in winter when snow was stuck to the grass, intimately. One light thing moved through something that was solid, darker. In that moment, someone had asked me to help host a festival of literature.

"Yes," I had said.

"It will be about memory."

I was admiring what was underfoot.

THE BEAK OF A BIRD

Sometimes I forget the names of books, the ones I like the most. My memory is bad, and I'm also ashamed of what I think about literature—I can only open up to a few people in this way. I work in a bookstore, so this isn't a good quality.

After work, I walk home in the dark. Sometimes on the way I stop at a gourmet food shop, knowing I don't belong there, and yet feeling that I do. I buy a small jar of something, like pumpkin butter, and I have a friend, a cousin, who likes to come over after she's finished working at the hotel. She's young and so working at the hotel doesn't bother her. I am already too old to be able to work at a hotel, though I did work at one once, and I am only a few years older than her. We come from a long line of women who have worked in hotels.

I clean my apartment until it's immaculate so that it feels like a good place to be, a kind of nest for when my cousin comes to visit. A place safe from this rich city, though we play at a certain kind of richness. Once I slapped my cousin so hard she fell down. It was because of something that had happened in our family, and I know now I was wrong. She forgave me. In our family we are good at that.

When I was a child I thought no one had experienced the world like I had. I would sit next to the ocean and think, no one knows the ocean like I do. No one has ever been this close to it. I didn't actually say these things in my mind, I just knew them to be true. My connection to the ocean; my walk through the tropical night. If I walked long enough I came to farmland.

One night when I was working in the bookstore my cousin called to tell me she had hurt herself at the hotel.

"What happened?" I asked.

"I cut myself with a pair of scissors. One of the customers left them under a towel on the bathroom floor. I didn't know the scissors were there. Now my hand won't stop bleeding."

"Clarice, tell your manager. Don't just let your hand bleed."

"Okay, I'll tell him."

"There must be a first aid kit at the hotel."

"There is. I've seen it. Once I had to get a band aid for someone."

"How bad is your hand?"

"Not that bad. It just startled me. I didn't know I was going to get cut when I picked up the towel."

"Should I come get you?"

"When your shift is over."

At nine o'clock, after I had closed out my register and put the money in the safe, I left the store and headed north toward the hotel. It was a cold night and I crossed my arms in front of me, trying to keep my body warmth close. The streets were dark until I got to the one the hotel was on. Then everything was bright. My cousin was standing out front, cradling one hand in another. She was wearing a puffy beige coat that came down to her knees, a coat I had never seen before.

"Are you okay?"

"One of the other maids wrapped my hand for me. It isn't bleeding anymore."

I looked at Clarice's hands. The one on top looked thick under its thin glove. "Do you need stitches?"

"I don't think so."

"Let's take the bus tonight."

The bus was bright too. We went to the back row and spread ourselves out over four seats. No one else was riding, but after a few stops two people got on, and then every few minutes a few more. One woman was wearing a coat like Clarice's, except that it was falling apart.

When we got into my apartment, Clarice leaned against the kitchen wall and stayed there.

"Don't worry," she said, "I'm okay. It just feels good to stand here."

I made up a bed for Clarice on the couch, and then climbed into my own bed. I could hear the music she turned on in the living room, but it sounded very far away. She must have only wanted to hear it quietly. I lay in bed, listening. I fell asleep. Then it was time to go to the bookstore. When I got up, Clarice was already gone.

It didn't take long to see her again. That night we were less tired, and we decided to eat at a nice restaurant, one that serves crepes. Clarice went on and on about her injury and about one of the other maids, and I recounted my time as a child when I had visited the tropics.

"I am on someone's farm," I said. "You can imagine how strange a farm seems, especially when it is tropical. The air is so warm that I don't need to wear a flannel shirt or a sweater. It's so beautiful I don't want to go to sleep." Clarice stared at me. Because we were cousins we could go on and on about things that other people would ignore or object to. "I was an only child," I said. "Clarice, is it funny the way I talk about these things? It must be boring."

"I don't mind it."

"It was my consciousness I was aware of. I was always looking at things, like my own body. When I was walking I would touch my body in amazement because I could walk. I would touch the muscles in my legs."

"I know you were an only child," Clarice said.

"It means something to me."

"What does it mean?"

I paused. Then I went on. "I was alone more of the time. I was alone much more than you were."

"That's true. When I was growing up, I was always with my brother."

"What's it like having a brother?"

"Can't you imagine it?"

"I guess I did see you together. You seemed tense."

Clarice stared down at her soup. Then she ate some of it. Her orange soup. "I don't think I told you, but last week I saw a performance."

"Do you go to performances?"

"One of the other maids took me."

"What was it like?"

"There were four dancers, and it seemed like they didn't actually know how to dance."

"You don't really know what dancing looks like, do you?"

"Not contemporary dance, but I know what ballet looks like."

After that conversation, I think we both needed a break from each other. I spent a whole day reading a book in my kitchen. I knew I would never be able to talk to anyone about it. I washed the dishes. While I was doing that, I finished the conversation in my mind that I had had with Clarice.

"What were you doing on the farm?" she asked me.

"I had gone there because of the ocean. Also, I am an only child."

"What does being an only child have to do with it?"

"You find you must do what you want."

"Do you? I don't know very much about only children."

"We're very aware of everything, and also sometimes afraid."

I made myself stop the conversation. I sat down at the table and started reading again so that the words I read would fill my mind.

The next morning I went to work and it didn't stop raining. In between shelving books I would stand in front of the large windows and stare out at the parking lot. People came and went, running from their cars to our store, or sometimes to another store across the street.

"Don't forget where you are," the assistant manager said to me.

The hours crept slowly by. When a customer asked me a question I answered it quickly so I could be alone again.

One customer got angry with me because I was reading when she walked up to the cash register, and I didn't notice her. She said to one of the other employees that it didn't even seem as if I cared about books. I thought this was odd because I had been holding a book and looking down at it when she saw me. But in a way she was right—I didn't care.

At the hotel, Clarice found a piece of something that looked like a miniscule rock or a piece of gray coral. She took it to a natural food store because she wasn't sure how else she could find out what it was. It wasn't food, but people who worked in a store like this might know.

"It's a fulgurite," she later told me. We were on the bus again, it was night, and I felt like we could have been anywhere.

"How do you know?"

"The food store. And then I looked it up online. It's formed when lightning hits sand."

"Everything in this city is so ugly that I can't focus on my life."

"There are things here that are beautiful."

"Like what?" I asked.

"Our friendship, for one thing."

"But we're cousins."

"Okay, then our family."

She dragged me along to an old brownstone that is owned by the historical society. In one room, a glass pitcher had been placed in a clear glass box and set on top of a pedestal along with four small cups. "Is this hand blown?" I asked.

"Everything in this room is hand blown."

What were all of these hand blown things here for? What were we supposed to think about when we looked at them? Next we walked into a bedroom. There was a bed with a green and red bedspread on top of it, and a wooden headboard against pink and white wallpaper from another time. Above the bed was a painting. "Snow scene of a courtesan holding an umbrella being ferried across the Sumida River by a porter," Clarice read out loud. In the painting, the porter wore something that covered his head and face, like a dust mop made out of soft straw. The brown river water surrounded the boat, moving toward it in little waves.

"Do you like this place because a rich family once lived here?" I asked her. I knew I was being ridiculous, but I couldn't stop myself from saying it.

"No, I just like it."

"Why?"

"What does it matter to you?"

Out on the balcony of the house, Clarice's open coat billowed around her in the wind. She had gone out there to take a break from me, and I watched her looking at the city, an ugly city that seemed to have no end.

THE SLEEVE OF MY COAT

We have gotten into the habit of inviting other couples to our house to play cards, and once they are here they stay for a long time. I am always surprised by it. At five A.M. one would expect to be in bed, sleeping. They relax here, maybe too much. It might be that they feel relaxed by how close we are to the ocean.

In the afternoons everything happens that can't happen at night. Time. Food. A toy horse that races across the living room floor when my neighbor comes to visit with her children. We sit on the terrace ever so tensely. Almost transparent, like the tip of a plant.

For a long time I couldn't get settled in life. I remember this constantly. I think about it on the terrace. I would see a dog and think it was a cat. Then something got bigger. My personality.

In between visits from the couples, and the neighbor and her children, my husband and I work in our studies. My husband's study is filled with tropical plants, which he keeps warm in the winters with fluorescent lights. My study is filled with books and dust. I like working when I know he is also working. I hear him watering his plants, and smoking. Sometimes I'm extremely frustrated when I write, and in other moments I am extremely scared. I never knew it was possible to be scared while working on a story.

One night in my study I felt I was supposed to write about our house. I had never before seen our house as a strange thing. I looked at the clothes in my closet. I knew that this was writing, to look at those clothes. Later, when the couples arrived, I was distant from them.

Tonight it seems like fall, but it isn't. In the kitchen my husband is making a very involved salad. We sit talking about our work, and eating, and I drip olive oil onto my blouse, accidentally.

"Your face is flushed," my husband says.

Something croaks loudly at the window, startling me.

I will never write a novel. I will never write about the couples. I will *know* the couples. I will know myself.

"What's wrong?" my husband asks.

"There's always someone here. When am I supposed to write?"

After dinner I go into one of the rooms of the house. Sitting in a chair, an antique, I feel—enormous. My personality. Mixed with fall.

My husband is calling me from somewhere upstairs. It sounds as if he is in a hallway. I get interested in my own breath, which doesn't happen very often. The curtain moves, and I like the way it matches something inside me. But I know that a curtain shouldn't match me, and that I shouldn't like it.

Morning arrives and I drag myself out of bed hours after my husband has gotten up. The room is cold and airy, but I don't care: today there's something nice about it. I want to air out my mind. I find a pair of pale yellow tights in one of the drawers of our dresser.

"You idiot," I say to them.

But I go outside wearing the yellow tights all the same and find my neighbor's daughter playing with a huge stuffed animal on our terrace.

"What's that?" I ask.

"A rhinoceros," says Sylvie. She's wearing a black leotard and tutu, and grabbing onto the banister she pulls herself along it. She doesn't look like she's dancing, but she does seem to be enjoying herself.

I ask her, because I do want to know, "Is that dancing?" and she says that it is, that she learned it the day before in her ballet class. "It's *not* dancing," I tell her and she doesn't respond. Just like with the couples, I'm surprised at how long this "dancing" can go on, but I try to stay present.

It's the kind of morning that's more like an evening it's so dark outside. A newspaper blows along the street. I feel something towards it. A tree limb sways up and down in the breeze.

Outside I can see my past. Here is where I stood with a friend and talked about a movie. Here is the exact moment I knew I wanted to write. Here's the bed I slept in with someone I once loved. Here is the weather when I had bronchitis. Here is the emotion when I said goodbye.

That night I drink five glasses of wine, even though I usually only drink one. With five glasses of wine, I begin to admire my life. All these attractive couples are around me. How did it happen?

"I made lentil soup," I hear one of the men say, as he deals cards around a table. It makes me realize I have no idea what the couples do when they are not at our house.

There is my husband. He's been with the same couple all night. I begin to admire him, the way the couple is very easily in his presence. I am usually rigid, and though many couples approach me, I have a hard time allowing them to stay. I make my excuses and go out to the terrace. I look down at the grass. Inevitably a couple comes and sits with me quietly. This is the kind of couple I am most suited for.

When we try to sleep that night my husband is like a dog or a cat, and I'm unsettled by it.

"A couple came upstairs," he says.

"When?"

"After you had five glasses of wine."

"What did they do up here?"

He paws at the darkness. "They wanted to see your study."

"What did they think about it?"

"They said they felt at home."

The next day it's warm again, as it should be. The ocean is calm and it looks as if a shark will come out of it. Then my neighbor appears.

"What's wrong?" she asks.

"When I look at you I see a character from a book."

"I am not a character."

"You are. An annoying one."

She doesn't leave. The water moves through its waves. "It's you who looks like a character."

"Which one?"

"The one who—." She stops. "Dies."

At home I ask my husband, "Where's our neighbor's husband?" I am sitting in his study among his tropical plants. There are so many of them. One plant blocks out one couple.

"I think he left."

The couples and my neighbor and her children, I write in my notebook.

"What are you writing?" my husband asks me.

"It's too new to share."

"Are you worried she's lonely?"

"No. Will you play some music? Something pretty."

He plays something stressful.

I like having to wear tights under my dress. It's because of something inside me. Their hair blowing back lightly from their faces. You'll never understand how angry I am. Today the plants are like a painting. It's not a cry to writing, it's a cry to a future novel. Always ignoring her. People have fucked in here. Here is a novel in which—I know them in a certain kind of way. Sylvie has picked up a rhinoceros and is hitting it against a wall.

"You're writing in my study."

"Is it okay?"

"Of course, you're my wife."

"When the couple's in my study, can I be here?"

"Don't you want to be in your study with them, to make sure they don't mess anything up?"

THEY'VE BEEN BRINGING THEM HERE FOR DECADES

"Can you see?"

"No, it's too dark."

"Hang on to this railing."

"It's so desolate here, like a corral. It feels like I'm holding on to something people tie their horses to."

"It's true. People bring their horses here. They've been bringing them here for decades."

What were we doing in a corral? I had agreed to spend time with my friend; I hadn't agreed to be in a place I couldn't see. Lately he had been doing versions of this, asking me to participate in one thing or activity, and then putting me in another situation. I should have been used to it, but I wasn't. To be in this place in the horses' absence was . . . what? My friend knew this; it was why he had brought me here.

I tried to take everything in; I tried to be in this place. I think my friend wanted us to be in the place without talking, but I wanted to talk, so I did. "Last night I went to a dinner party," I said.

"Really?"

"Really. The table was set up outside in the grass, not far from a hive. We sat there; we ate. There was a conversation about a book I had actually just read, but I didn't join in."

"Why not?"

"I liked listening. I thought it was such a nice coincidence, a long conversation about a book I had just finished; it was as if something or someone had brought this to me, said after you are done there will be a conversation for you to listen to."

"Who would've brought it?"

"That doesn't matter. After dinner I went to look at the hive and saw the bees flying in the air. They were so small. It was dark out by that time, but not as dark as it is now."

I turned to my friend, but I couldn't see him. I could see a shape of him. I stuck my hand out and hit his sleeve.

"What is the book about?"

We could see each other now; we faced each other, at a table. Lights were on.

"It's about a man and a woman who spend time together, but in a way that most of us don't spend time. He is repulsed by her because she is a woman. She doesn't care; she wouldn't trade their kind of relationship for another. Can I read some of it to you?"

I took the book from my bag: "The woman says, 'it suits her very well, what she's going through with him now. She wonders what she would have done instead if they hadn't met in the cafe. It's here in this room that she's had her real summer, her experience, her encounter with hatred of her own sex, and of her body, and of her life.'"

"Did you like it?"

"I loved it."

"What did the people at the dinner party say about it?"

"They thought it was funny."

"How is it funny?"

"The female character puts black silk over her face and says she's a writer. Listen to this part: 'One night she asks him if he could do it with his hand, but without coming close to her, without even looking. He says he couldn't. He can't do anything like that with a woman. He can't even say how he feels about her having asked. If he agreed, he might not want to see her any more, ever. He might even hurt her.' But he wants her to be there, every night, just lying in that room. Just lying there."

"Would you like to be in that situation?"

"Yes. Well, I don't think I would like it while it was happening, but afterwards I would."

"Why after?"

"Because from that safe distance I could appreciate what had happened."

"What do you think would happen?"

"I would be intimate with someone in a new way. Or, I would at least recognize our time together as intimate, admit to its qualities of intimacy. I would experience those qualities."

"Is lying in a room every night intimate, if you and the other person are strangers, aren't even attracted to each other, and are possibly even repulsed?"

"It's intimate because of the repulsion."

"I don't know if I see that as intimate."

Later it was dark again. I thought I could hear the faint sounds of something, some animal, drinking water. I imagined its tongue making contact with the water. "Can you hear that?"

"No, I don't hear anything. I think I was asleep. Aren't you tired?"

My challenge is to relax with another person in the way I relax when no one is there. Sometimes I can't let go when I'm with my friend. Some part of me stays stiff, and then that stiffness seems to expand over the whole surface of my body, even when I am moving.

Again I listened for the water, but I couldn't hear it anymore. I thought, It's already gone. Then I thought, Let yourself go.

I said out loud: "I'm trying to relax."

"Is it working?"

"Yes, but if you weren't here it would be easier."

"Should I leave?"

"No, that would be a failure."

Relax, like the animal relaxes when it is drinking water. Relax, like I relax when I drink water. "Once you took me to a movie. This was years ago, when we first met."

"I remember."

"On the way to the movie it was windy, but the wind was warm. On the freeway, our hair blew around our faces. I remember the inside of your car, which was messy. From the lights on the dashboard I could see all the things you'd thrown on the floor. For me you hadn't shaped yourself into a full person yet. You were someone I could introduce myself to. I know how to do that."

"Do you know how to stay friends with someone for a long time?"

"I'm not sure."

That night, while we lay in bed after we had finally stopped talking, I had a vision. Someone went crazy in a community, but was supported by everyone and everything around her. In the vision, the support was palpable in the green grass people walked through to get to wherever it was they were going. I could see her. And I knew she could see me.

WORDS COME TO ME

Even though I don't write stories I create them in my actions. I create a feeling I don't believe in and then I act on that feeling. I wear my puffy coat out into the snow. I walk through my neighborhood and look at the antique shops. Snow and antiques are good together. I sit in a warm place to read.

The one time in my life I had to escape from something, I created a story about the longest February of my life.

Here, I want to show you something; it is several cats.

Like a creature that won't get down from the bed, words are coming to me.

Here I am on the street with so many people. It's beautiful to be alive, to go into a floral shop in winter and look at fine plants sitting darkly in their pots. To be among a crowd hurts me.

"Let me see this plant," I say to the florist. And she lets me look at it for quite some time while she works in the back. It's strange how long I stay there.

Now words come to me. I have not asked them. Sighing, I take my notebook out of my puffed pocket and write the words down in my best hand. Though I will never be a writer, the words allow me to study a certain kind of writing. If I close my eyes I will see my written self staring back at me. If I walk to the lake something will be revealed in the waves frozen up in their certainty. Did I tell you the waves freeze here? I will feel something I don't actually feel. Then I will fall asleep in my bed like the waves.

So much happens when I am inside my mind, but I still haven't left the floral shop. I have not left the fine plants.

Remember when I was kidnapped by our "master" and forced to be a part of his life in a way I never would have wished for? He took me to a dairy farm, expecting me to like it. He took me to a fancy party where the other women looked at me with rage and jealousy. How could they want that life?

My notebook is too modern. When I hold it up next to myself it contrasts greatly. Still, I am safe now. To look at antique furniture in shop windows instead of sitting on it. To know that no one will handcuff me to a wrought iron gate.

My desk is waiting for me. Softly, softly, the books. In my apartment, I draw the bathwater. I've been outside all day, with people, and now it is time for me to be alone. Taking baths has always been important for me, especially in winter. I am more receptive then. I can feel myself going out, and then coming back in. It's hard not to feel connected to yourself when you're in a hot bath.

I had good friends; I had you. We served food to the family we "worked" for. When you set the table or ladled out the soup, I looked at you lovingly. I looked at all of you this way. I wasn't able to stop myself from doing it. Once I was beaten for standing there doing nothing while everyone else worked. "It's just that I really wanted to see them," I said during the beating.

The bath warms me. I will be able to emerge into the room as a warm person.

"They're not your real friends," my master's wife said. Our "mistress."

It's too late, I thought. I know the warmth of love. I watched her pink face while she beat me. Then she pushed me onto the floor. Down there, all I had were pointy black shoes to look at. I hadn't realized how many people, how many shoes, were in that room.

When you lie in a field with a friend and tell each other stories about your lives—when you have explored friendship—it's impossible to forget. It comes back when you're lying on a cold floor.

It comes back when you're lying in the bath.

Lovingly, Juliet, blank page, edited by Anne, women of the rural areas. This is written on a piece of paper on my desk. If you sit in my chair and look down at my notebook my words are waiting for you.

Myself, alone, in my bed, is a story.

What direction did you head in when we scattered from that house, like the bits of dry grass that we were?

I read books now to bring myself to a feeling. When I walk down the street I'm never sure if I interact with others, or if they interact with me.

I eat warm food, things other people wouldn't consider eating. Even in winter the waves unfreeze, falling upon the cold beach. I wear one color to signify something. It's been said that you can signal many things in this way, like the words you're most likely to write down, and even your education.

My bookshelves reach from the floor to the ceiling, towering over my small apartment. A table sits in front of the shelves. This is where I prepare my food. The kitchen and the living room are practically the same. I want you to know where I am, what I look like when I am here. I want you to see what I look like when I eat.

Another time I was beaten, I was sick with the flu. Our mistress held me down while our master whipped me with his belt. This happened on the porch because she wanted their neighbors to see us. It was December and I was shivering magnificently. Later, our master spoke to me in hushed tones.

He said, "Next week I'll take you out again, when you're better. Would you like to listen to music? We can go to the mountains."

He always played music with banjos in it. He was always trying to soothe me. The only one who could was another servant.

Only once did I see you being beaten. It was because you had tried to leave the house without permission. Our mistress asked a male servant to beat you, and he did. What else could he have done? Bloody, you sat on the back steps while a kitten tried to crawl up your leg. You let it, but you didn't acknowledge its presence. I stood in the window looking out at you for a long time. Finally it got dark, and then I couldn't see you anymore.

Those years hardly resemble this one, or the ones in which I was a child, but all of it equals my life, making one ragged crawl across time.

Now it's morning. Here I am on a walk to the lake. This is real. I wear headphones to clear out the feeling I had in the night, and to change the lake to a softer place. I listen to music that helps me understand something about myself and about the lake. I want to understand the food I eat. And why I like antiques and snow.

Someone told me that writers are more important to me than they are to other people. Oddly, they were important to the people who owned that house, and I'm still trying to reconcile that. Once, in their winter, our mistress hung a laurel wreath on the front door. I had always found that door beautiful, with its wood and glass, its richness. With the wreath its beauty deepened and this made me feel sick.

I'll buy something simple for my own door, from the floral shop that is warmer and brighter than any house I've been in.

I am trying to show the mind.

I cannot write anything else except sentences.

QUEEN

Marguerite, cleaning a room. Me, falling on the ice, taking some kind of mild drug, being separated by a rope. Sometimes I feel like I am being held back by this rope, as if everywhere I go I am separated from what I see. Cleaning next to Marguerite, a strange excitement. We go into different rooms. I get bored. The next morning walking to work again, an ice storm. It's six o'clock. Everything separated by ice, for everyone, separated, not just for me. I wish you didn't have to work so hard. I like being a maid. Though I am collecting dirt, I feel like I am being washed all the time. This hotel. Something inside me.

I strip the sheets off the bed, throw them on the floor. In the next room she says, once in a while I have to take this. I want to know why I am like that. The ice displays branches, wires, pieces of grass, even the beak of a bird. I am looking at the beak of a bird. Did it die in the storm? Objects. The tiny cameo necklace my grandmother gave me. Something Marguerite gives me, on paper. Keep it in your pocket, she says. I touch a wall. Make dinner for Marguerite. Eat quietly. A lamp on the wooden table. An album with sounds of geese, and then wolves howling. Eight o'clock. Dinner long over, but Marguerite won't go home.

Let me read to you. Let me wash your feet. I stiffen up; then I let her. It doesn't stop snowing. The water sends a chill up my spine. I start to cry. Why are you crying? Is it time for spring? Not quite. Still winter. Cut my stomach, accidentally. Wave after wave of pleasure. The warm water. My feet. Painting of one hundred women. Their heads are missing. How do you know what they are? Put dishes away. Wipe off the table. Thank you, Marguerite. You're welcome. Keep this. You'll need it. I like to think I don't need anything. It's not true. Take this black ribbon. Wrap it around my eyes. Marguerite plays the sound of a storm. Next to it is the storm outside. I sit next to the heating vent.

I feel comfortable. But I know someone is making tracks outside. If something changes, I'll beg for it to stay the same. Last week at the library I just stood there, witnessing myself and another, shamed. You don't have to work again until Monday. You can go home and hide yourself. I always thought you'd do something else with your life. But it's this. I don't mind. Channeling, I think about my grandmother. We always knew we were the same person. Are we? One maid turns into another. Exchanges form. Night. Ten o'clock. Wave after wave washes over us. Someone is making tracks. Monday comes more quickly than I thought it would. Five o'clock. I wake up, it's still dark, put on my clothes, start walking. Something clean in the air.

At the hotel, flapping the towels. Collecting laundry for the linen service. I slide down the wall and sit on the floor. What are you doing, asks Marguerite. It's not time for a break yet. The boss is gone. No one will see me. I vacuumed right when I got here. What does vacuuming have to do with it? Today everything is normal. I could shame Marguerite, and I wouldn't care. I don't understand, she says. The empty hallways of the hotel become crowded. So many people are staying here. From behind his newspaper, a man watches me. Overcast sky. Painting of a river scene, children with kites. I still don't understand. Everything is frozen. It's winter. Tramps everywhere.

Night to myself. Read. Walk. I managed to get a book. And always, cleaning to be done. Play music. The woman's voice. Scrub the bathtub. Mop the floor. Fall into bed. Stay still. Queen. How many are walking around out there? Like people. Like ghosts. Try to find a pencil. Draw all over my arm. Read again. Nine o'clock. "Forgive me if I add something more about myself since my identity is not very clear, and when I write I am surprised to find that I possess a destiny. Who has not asked himself at some time or other: am I a monster or is this what it means to be a person?"

TRAMPS EVERYWHERE

A woman walks through bright lights.

The same woman limps down a road.

It is Mary Lebyatkin.

A horse-drawn carriage thunders down another dusty road. Mary stops and listens.

INT. Night. A drawing room. There is an oval mirror on the wall, and under it a table. The other walls are smudged. In the middle of the room are a sofa and two chairs. Mary sits in one of the chairs, soaking her feet in a small tub. She massages them.

Bedroom. A single oil lamp on a table next to a bed. Mary reads a book. Another woman lies in bed with Mary, also reading. White legs. Brown legs.

One of Mary's feet is propped up. It is huge.

The camera focuses in on the windowpane, to the night.

The next shot is identical to the first, but the other woman isn't there. The camera stays and watches Mary.

Mary blows out the oil lamp. Darkness.

EXT. Morning. Strong sun. Short and long shots of a swamp. A closeup of a frog. It sits on the bank then jumps into the water, making circles on the surface. The camera stays, looking at the swamp.

Voiceover: I walked into the day.

INT. Night. Mary is dressed for the opera. A black bodice and a colorful feather in her hair. We can't see her foot, but it seems to pulse. Beside her is a man. It is Nikolai Stavrogin. Both watch the stage.

Flashback: Mary and Nikolai in the drawing room. The music is still audible. Mary and Nikolai scream at each other, but it is the opera we hear. Nikolai sweeps the things on a table onto the floor. Mary limps toward the camera.

INT. Night. The opera house. The same scene as before. No trace of the fight between Mary and Nikolai.

EXT. Night.

Voiceover: The day like a mouth, and me in it.

The screen is quiet and dark.

Nikolai: Do you want to know why I married you?

Mary: No.

Nikolai: I lost a bet.

Gradually the screen lightens, just enough to see the two of them sitting near the swamp. Nikolai reaches for Mary, but she pulls away. As the viewer, you barely see this. It is still too dark. Mary does something else, but it is still too hard to see.

Mary: I want some food.

This scene is longer than it seems.

EXT. Day. A crowded market.

Voiceover: Here, I find what I need to exist.

The camera zooms in on various vegetables. A zucchini, an ear of corn, squash.

Voiceover: All of this food, who is it for? Why has no one given it to me?

Mary is seen limping next to the stalls of vegetables. We see her look at and want what she sees. We see a close-up of her face. It is dirty.

Voiceover: When Nikolai said "we will be married now," I was confused. He is rich, and sometimes I fall down when I walk. My foot is bigger than everyone else's. But I know things other people don't.

The camera follows Mary as she pays a woman for a small basket of apples. We hear her conversation with the woman, blended into the sounds of the market.

The film flashes back to a scene of a violent thunderstorm, to an oil lamp flickering inside a window. A horse whinnies in terror.

Voiceover: I know the sound of the wind knocking down a ravaged animal.

We see Mary running out into a field. A horse falls down. Mary holds onto its neck and falls with it.

We see her again at the market. She is limping down the street.

Voiceover: I know how to bring the animal back to life.

INT. Night. Drawing room. Mary and the woman who was in bed with her are sewing. They sit in the two chairs. They sew together old pieces of scrap. It is everywhere.

Woman: What will you do if Nikolai tries to kill you?

Mary doesn't stop. She continues sewing. She seems determined to sew.

Voiceover: I've been pricked by a needle many times. And if I had all of those pricks at once?

Woman: What's wrong, Mary?

Mary: I don't want to die.

Outside the window, we see a horse-drawn carriage drive past. It moves slowly, almost like it is floating. The camera stays with the carriage; one part, and then another. A horse's head, and then a man's hand holding the reins, and then a wheel, and then the back of the carriage that is moving out of view.

Voiceover: I'll take anything life has to give me, even if it's been trampled and crushed.

INT. Night. Drawing room. The soundtrack is silent while Mary is beaten. It is Nikolai who is beating her. He beats her for a long time.

INT. Bedroom. Mary inside an armoire, crying. She strokes her foot. There is still no sound.

Voiceover: I'll take anything.

EXT. Day. Mary and Nikolai in the back of a carriage. They stare ahead. Mary's hair is messed up. Nikolai holds onto a balloon. He kills her.

Voiceover: Is this what it means?

EXT. Evening. Short and long shots of chickens in a yard. We watch them walk around, pecking at pieces of sewn-together cloth. The camera focuses in on a chicken's bright pink comb.

We see Mary, sitting on the ground. She crawls to a water trough. She puts her hand in it. She starts yelling. Then she drinks.

INT. Evening. A crowded inn. Mary sits alone at a table, eating. There is corn on her plate. The camera zooms in on it, focuses on Mary, then on the other people and objects in the room. A man's shoe, a woman's hat, a huge piece of bread. The scene becomes blurry. From across the room Mary's only friend walks toward her. Mary stands up and limps into the night.

THE BEATING OF MY HEART

She is lame because one of her legs is shorter than the other. It is noticeably so. She hobbles around. She has no money for food. She begs for food. Someone gives her a head of lettuce, but it has bugs in it. It takes a long time to rinse the bugs out of the lettuce. She eats the lettuce. She feels grateful.

They make a play about her life, though when it is finally performed she is dead. She died because one of her feet got infected. Every night, gingerly, she had tried to clean it. An actress sits in the middle of the stage. Her foot is huge. Her dress is all torn up and there are smudges on her face. A faint smile too.

His parents gave him everything they had, and then he gave most of it to an orphanage. When he arrived at the orphanage, the children beat pots and pans. The rest of his money he burned up in a desert wash. He wanted to be a tramp. He wanted to never know where he was. Everything else felt wrong.

She decided to go out walking, even though it would take her a long time. A buggy passed. When it passed, she watched the muscles moving in the horses' legs. She listened to the clopping sounds of their feet on the ground. She listened to her own clopping sounds as she walked. She looked down at her muddy shoes. This is who I am, she thought. It doesn't matter what I'm wearing or what my feet sound like. What matters is this dusty road, and me on it. I'm hungry, but I'm sure that by the end of the day I'll find food.

I don't want this money anymore. I want to see if I can feed myself from what I find on the ground. I want to eat plants and wild mushrooms, but I'll have to learn about mushrooms to make sure I don't eat poison. I'll have to figure out which plants are safe. With the little money I have left I'll buy a book. From now on this book will help me find food.

In a play I am a poor woman. I have smudges on my face. My foot is huge. I walk home, wiping makeup off my face. I study everything around me. I don't take off the foot, for it is the meaning of my life. I fall down, and then I stay down, laughing hysterically. I don't want this to end.

If I do a thing I don't want to do, will I have enough money to pay for a room? Will I be a different person, a person who does something like this? Will my insides change? When you look at me what will you see? And what will I see when I look at you?

What will you do with your life, with your money? Where will you go? There is almost nothing to stop you now. If you want this, you should live it.

She walks through the dark city and there are lights everywhere. She is almost blinded by them. Is this what it means to absorb and be absorbed by the night? If I am myself, am I also a dog who is dying? Am I a person being shot in the head? Am I making love to my own shadow? What is this place?

This is the place where your life unfolds. You push something back so the other thing can come forward. This thing is anything, or it is nothing, and you see it be nothing.

I am the reflection of someone who is dying. When I am looked at, it's not me that is seen. I am a giant mirror. You are too. See that woman lying down in the road? When you are in front of her, she is reflected in your eyes.

To become a giant mirror, to stand in the middle of the wind knowing that's all you are.

The lame one hobbles to her destiny.

Time opens up and you don't know what you're seeing. Or how anyone feels.

I want someone to love me. I want someone to take care of my feet. I want someone to wash my feet in rosewater and wrap them in warm towels. I work hard and every part of me is stiff. I want everyone to remember that I had feet and they carried me everywhere. I want everyone to remember that when I was with the rich, I kissed their hands and laughed hysterically.

He is the only one in his family who has seen this place and its creatures. From the light of his lantern he crosses the land that rises in front of him. In a small town someone gives him a gold watch he would like to refuse, but he takes it. Now he has two things to hold. I'm hungry because I haven't eaten in weeks. Something inside me is doubling over. I'm all alone now, but this is the way I wanted it.

Time opens up and something is wrong. The wind blows in the opposite direction. The sky is a strange color. Even my voice sounds like someone who hasn't spoken in a long time.

When I rehearse, I don't have to memorize my lines. The auditorium holds my thoughts and all I have to do is step into them. I am getting closer and closer to something, but I don't know what it is. Only that it is here. On my dress. In the air. When it is not my turn to be on stage I sit in the wings, and think, and sew.

Tonight I'll eat bugs. I won't complain because it's all I have. The days are getting longer. Someone said hello to me on my walk. Soon, I'll only feel pleasure.

GENTLE NIGHTS

When people look at me they sometimes think of the word "decadence," but I only have the face and body of a decadent person, not the experience. I am someone who enjoys getting rid of things, even if it seems like I should be sitting down in a jewelry store surrounded by gold.

Something has brought me here. Violent paintings. Almost all of them are religious. Here, in the middle of the gallery, is that famous one of St. John the Baptist's head on a platter. See the shadows on Salome's face and neck? When I see too many paintings like this, I emerge into something softer, allowed the pleasure of arriving from a museum into a warm winter night. This is why I look. Snow blankets the ground, but not coldly. I could take off my coat if I wanted to. I don't have to wear gloves.

Usually I gravitate toward paintings of village scenes. Look at this one with its bright dabs of light in the windows of the houses. I would like to go inside the houses. I would like to go inside those rooms above the pastry shop. In one of the windows sits a simple striped chair and a side table with books on top. I could read in that room, and entertain guests.

Even though I am not a decadent person, I have had decadent friendships. I have been able to love many people. Today I miss everyone and I look at the paintings feeling near to something.

I have been trying to figure out my relationship to the person I live with, who I also love, though I don't know him very well. We have only lived together for a few weeks and in that time there have been many nights of sitting bundled up on the porch, and now that it's even colder, in the living room or the kitchen, or one of us reads in bed. It is me who usually lies in bed, sometimes with my laptop. I look at things on the Internet, but I am still aware of the mountains around us. They have become part of everything and the Internet doesn't stop this.

Here is a winter scene in which a shrub covered in snow looks like a tarantula. And a painting of a frost fair on the river Thames in 1684. A full marketplace set up for the freezing, the doors of the tents flapping, and people riding over the ice on their horses to get to them, or walking in groups of three or four, with a dog running on ahead. In this painting the light comes from a small fire on the edge of the frozen river.

Here I am returning home. My figure crosses the landscape; a mountainside with dark houses perched here and there. Now I am on the porch, stamping the snow from my boots. The person I live with is heating something on the stovetop.

We embrace. The room is warm from the stove.

"You look like you want something," he says.

"It's just the way my face is shaped." The living room is sparse and perfect. Two comfortable chairs with an oval rug between them. A clear glass bowl sits on the windowsill. All the boxes are gone.

"It looks great in here," I say. "Actually, it might be the best place I've ever lived in."

"Me too."

"I'll go organize the bedroom."

All of our bedroom things are taken out of boxes, cleaned, and put away; when your belongings are few, unpacking doesn't take long. The bed is next to the window, and now there's a fine dresser across from it that used to belong to my grandmother. Our clothes are inside. I place pink and blue cloth flowers in my hair and see my reflection. I'm startled by how spoiled I look.

Before I left the last city I lived in, all my friends had already moved. I went to a party and in the bathroom I thought to myself, when you walk back out none of the people you love will be there.

One friend is too much in her body, and was one of the people I missed most in that bathroom, feeling how far away she was, that I wouldn't go with her to parties in that city anymore. Another friend and I used to remind each other that someday this moment would be over, a continuous recognition, grateful to still be immersed in it.

For a long time after that I thought I had already met all the people worth meeting, but it wasn't true. Something in me has always been naïve, though I'm not sure my face has registered that.

Today I am going to the spa. It costs twenty dollars and I will spend five hours there. If only to warm up in winter, to sweat things out of me, I need the spa. In between the hot tub and the steam room I stay for a while in the cold pool just so I can get hot again.

Here is the mugwort tub, brewed like a tea. A sign above it lists its healing properties. One of them is for hysteria. Another is for tired legs. It's so hot I can barely lower myself all the way in, but I do. The black water laps at my collarbones.

Here is the dry sauna, glowing red, wide planks of wood lining the walls. Heated rocks rest elegantly in the corner, while a woman pours a pitcher of water on top of them. When I lie down, the wooden bench burns me. I am quieting something in myself.

With some of my friends I have had a falling out. In that bathroom, I also thought of them. I see myself as a caring person, but the anger directed at me from a few of the people I've been close to makes me question that characteristic. One friend said she had to end her relationship with me because I wasn't good for her. On the one hand this made sense, as I know there were ways in which I let her down. We were supposed to live with each other and I backed out of it. On the other hand it confused me, and made me feel as if I didn't know myself as well as I thought I did, because I loved her and I believed I had shown her this, in other ways. Maybe I'm not as in touch with the harmful parts of myself as I am with the loving. With some friends, we've taken turns hurting each other, and have come out of it on another side.

It's beautiful how long a friendship can last, even when it is awkward to be around each other. Even when there is nothing to say, neither person wants to let go. I think this is because the body still remembers the relationship, and most likely the bodies keep it alive in spite of the mind. The best thing would be to spend time with each other physically, but this is not always possible or appropriate.

The body remembers. The body wants to have its own relationship. The mind will have to say something about it afterward, or, sometimes the mind doesn't have to say anything at all.

Yesterday the person I live with bought me a richly designed dress, and though I like it very much, I'm afraid when I wear it I'll look aristocratic. It transforms me almost completely, physically that is. Paired with even a single piece of jewelry I'll barely know who I am.

"Try it on," he says.

In our simple, cabin-like house I put on a dress that is deeply, deeply patterned with the night sky.

I don't actually think I can look at myself in any kind of mirror.

We watch something violent on my laptop. It will help me wear this dress.

THERE'S AN EXCESS

There's an excess. I can see it around me. My skirt seems too black, my shirt too white. It's the same with the deep snow and the darkening sky.

I read all the time now, and the characters in the books I'm reading are clear and stark, like the one who marries because she mistakes love for study and learning, or else these things are better than love, or it is the only way she knows how to get close to the subjects she wants to know about. I know that this character is a better person than me. Though the religious scholar she marries is not as talented or charitable as she had first imagined, she remains dedicated to him regardless. I'm not religious but I want to be plain. As long as I am reading, this is true. I am austere. My husband thinks I am obsessed with myself.

"You are . . . I don't know," he says one night after dinner. It is nine o'clock.

"I must be hard to live with."

"It's not that, but you think about yourself too much. You're always doing self-analysis."

"I'm trying to figure something out."

There's an excess in him. He sits in front of the fireplace—very close to it—with three shirts on. Doesn't he get hot? His energy takes up so much room. It's almost as if he lives in the house more than I do, and yet I am the one who is always at home.

When we were traveling it rained constantly and he didn't seem to mind that either. We would get out of a train and walk in a downpour for five or ten minutes to see a palace or a fort. We would look at the palace in the downpour. Now I hate palaces and I hate forts. But I can be outside for a long time in winter, the lit windows of houses guiding me along, snow under my feet to tell me I am here. I come close to knowing things; I am allowed to feel things anyone would be lucky to feel. Even this is excessive.

At our house, large globes light the rooms. They are pleasing, their copper stems bending gracefully away from the wall. When my sister Maryrose comes to visit she polishes them. I tell her not to, but she insists. She is always trying to clean things. We are both probably too young to be married and our husbands too old. This is what my life has in common with literature.

"I feel empty tonight."

"Don't be sad," Maryrose says.

"Something is missing from here." We sit in great wingback chairs, observing each other. Maryrose is wearing a harsh outfit, not meant for this time. Her cheekbones are visible.

"You want too much."

"Maryrose, what do you see when you observe me?"

"Your kidneys."

"That's not fair." I turn around, so that my back is facing my sister. "What about now?"

"I still see them, from the front or from the back. It's what is visible in you right now, it's very clear."

When you spend your life looking at yourself in mirrors you don't know how to stop, when your face is wet, when you wake up in the middle of the night, when you're having a conversation with your husband.

Especially when I wash my face do I study it. When I am washing my face I listen to one song again and again, a very simple one. Everything I love is in this song. And then when I walk through the snow, Maryrose shows up beside me. She takes me to jewelry shops, and to perfumeries.

"Smell this one," she will say. "And this one."

Near us, other people are gathered around other scents.

The perfumer sprays a fragrance onto a small strip of paper and Maryrose bends to breathe it in. "Mmmm," she says.

"Let me smell it," I say. It is sweet and warm.

Then the perfumer walks behind the counter. On top of the counter burns a clean beeswax candle, its shadow on the wooden floor.

At home my husband says, "What is this? You've never worn perfume."

"Now I wear it."

"It's Maryrose. You spend too much time together."

"She's my sister."

"I know she's your sister."

"A sister is someone who changes you." Maryrose, in her long-sleeved shirt puffed at the shoulders.

"What is a husband then?" he asks angrily.

"Of course," I say. "A husband changes you too."

I brush my hair; I wear my favorite red dress; I go to the library to look for books. The librarians are afraid of me. I don't know why. The young ones and the old ones. When I walk next to the shelves or sit at a table with books spread around me, or even stand close to their desks, they steal glances at me constantly. I can't understand these attentions. And when I am right in front of them they'll hardly look at me at all. "It's because you let them," Maryrose says, but how could I control their eyes? It's too much.

"When you were a child," Maryrose says, "our mother had a hard time keeping you indoors. Every time she looked out the window there you were, playing with the dirt or a leaf. Even at night you were out in the leaves." What happened to me? A leaf is still beautiful, but it isn't interesting. "And where were you, Maryrose?" I ask her, because I can't remember. "Sometimes I was inside, and sometimes I wasn't home at all. When we were younger, we hardly spent time together."

When my husband gets home he asks, "Why are you always in bed? Are you sick?" He touches my forehead and brings a book to my side.

I take off my blouse and study my armpit and then my stomach.

"Is this your self-analysis?"

"It's part of it."

After dinner I hurry to Maryrose's. The cold air lifts off from the hills.

In my sister's living room I collapse into a chair next to the fireplace. "There's no vulnerability in you," she says before I've even had a chance to sink in.

"Of course there's vulnerability in me. There's everything in me."

"You don't have a real relationship to animals."

"I want to."

Maryrose is strange. She cradles my head next to her stomach, which I'm not sure I like. Her stomach is stranger still, hard. "You're going to have a baby."

"Do you want me to have a baby?" she asks.

"No."

"But I can't change it."

In the mirror above the fireplace, we are both flushed. We appear so alive. Maryrose in her gray dress, and me in the red dress I wear again and again. I watch myself press my face into her stomach. Leave through the top of your head.

FURNITURE, TABLE, CHAIR, SHELVES

There is a tone I want, but I don't know how to get it. A TONE IN MUSIC. I go to concerts (there are always concerts in the summer), trying to find something I can copy down or emulate. When I was a child I avoided music, but I have a very close connection to it now. I own a farm, but it's been a long time since I have DONE ANY WORK ON IT. I'm rich from my farm; I can do other things.

In the fields the crops grow almost too tall, their leaves reaching into the gentle air. This makes you question everything. What is air? What is gentle? Also, what is a child?

It is horrible to lose someone and yet that has happened to me. Now I'm alone, but I'm not unhappy. It is hot and beautiful enough on my farm that I feel okay about being rejected. I have tried to make other people reject me so I can relive my trauma in the way a person is supposed to live it. So far it hasn't happened, but JUST TODAY I SAW SOMEONE, and I think I can make this person do it. When I see this person I feel sick and I think this means I am on the right track.

This is something I concern myself with only in a "side pocket" sort of way. My priorities are with my compositions. I have thought about writing a farming manual, but I will have to think even more before I attempt it. I do write about my farm, but in a different way. I allow myself to inhabit my FARM poetically.

In the evenings I'm calm; I am hardly ever calm at any other moment. I wear what you think I would—long, flowing pants and a button-down denim shirt. My hair is either pulled back in a bun or pulled back with barrettes so that my hair hangs onto my shoulders. I used to be a dancer—you can see this in my posture and in the way I carry myself. I'm graceful. I know this and I'm not afraid to admit it for it is the great triumph of my life. Also, this helps me with music. Now that I no longer dance I WRITE MUSIC I think other dancers would enjoy. My compositions are complex and moody. They're not pretty, but they allow the listener a deeper relationship to my farm. At the end of the summer I will hold my own concert in this place.

My talents extend in every direction: farmer, possible writer of a farming manual, composer, dancer, possible musician. Now you understand why there is no time for me to actually farm.

Dressed in the way I've told you I stroll about the fields and often right off of them. The palm trees have their own relationship to air and it is exquisite to see. One can only imagine how their fronds take it in and change because of its presence. The movement is very slow. This slowness is good for me to witness. One part of a frond is pointing up, even while the rest of the points move to the left, or stay entirely still.

Then there is the river, moving in its own slow way. To watch the movement of the river sometimes means lying down next to it to GET CLOSE to the miniature swells and waves.

In the evenings when I am not strolling about I am in my house, cradled by the land. I sit down at my desk and work. I can't tell you what I look like when I'm working because I don't know. MY DESK IS HUGE AND BEAUTIFUL, very expensive, how could I not want to work there. The wood is unfinished, but in a particular kind of way. When it's touched it's smooth.

The compositions come easily, simply because I am cradled and I am able to express this through music. I am able to picture the dancers on the farm and compose songs that are right and true for them to dance to. I am waiting for the right time, for when I CAN HAVE A RECITAL HERE. I will have to work for months before this can happen, because I haven't yet matured into my craft. I haven't matured into any of them. But my relationship to everything I do is serious. You can't imagine how near I get to my work.

This person, the one with whom I would like to relive my rejection, is always in town. This person must live here now or at least be on a very long vacation. Sitting for hours in the café, not working at all. Or sometimes sitting in the rocking chair on the porch of the post office. But also, riding a bike or running along a path. This person is more relaxed than I am, but not healthier. No one in this area is healthier than me.

Imagine trying to compose something at the beginning of summer. Tonight I am an insect, a book, a VERY LARGE PLANT. Do you know what that's like? It means I am light, pensive, and then finally bigger than life. The one time I engaged in a sitting meditation my hands grew. They were huge. This was only a sensation. Here in this room I have enough love for everyone. Even the men (and the one woman) who work on my farm. There is something I want to get through to you, but I don't know how to do it. There is something I want to communicate about MY LIFE.

I have not always lived on this farm. I grew up in a city where I was taken everywhere I wanted to go. As a young woman I went to see aberrant things and this upset my family. I went to dance classes, where I was introduced to music. On cold autumn mornings the rain beat upon the windows and I exulted in my position in the class. I loved to dance. I even loved to wait on the floor until it was my turn to move across it.

Sometimes it is sensual just to be here, taking in the land, letting it wash over me. In certain moments I am a wild boar. I barely NEED ANOTHER.

At the first concert of the summer season I lie in the grass. Those closer to the stage sit in seats, and though I can afford to sit with them I prefer it here. I have always loved grass. The musicians are far away on the stage, but there are things about them that stand out all the same. They wear dark SKIRTS OR PANTS AND LIGHT shirts. They hold their instruments close to their bodies, or, if the instrument is on the ground they draw near it, hovering just above. I haven't yet put myself in the right proximity to an instrument. I have held a fiddle too far from my body.

The music is soft, then loud. Too loud. I look up at the sky. I had no idea it would be such a noisy concert and it hurts my ears. If I picture dancers now they are completely in crisis. They are violent criminals wearing costumes dyed a deep red. To picture this makes me nervous, as if I will be attacked before I get back to the farm. And of course there is nothing for me to copy down. When I hold a recital the music will be soft, so soft it will be hard to hear it. My talent lies in gentleness, even if I am not a gentle person.

Walking through the streets when the concert is over, the warm air pressing delicately against the night, I feel my future. The person I want to reject me is standing next to a palm.

"Hello," I call gently.

"What?" the person answers. The shadow of the PALM IS DEEP.

"It's so warm. And beautiful."

"It's always warm here."

"That's true. My farm is a bit farther down the road. Would you like to see it?"

This person takes so long to answer I'm afraid nothing will be said. But, finally, "I don't visit the farms of strangers."

I breathe out an audible sigh, like I have been taught to do in yoga, but I don't think this person understands anything like that. This person is gone before I know what's happened, leaving me completely alone. What I appreciate most about compositions, dance, and the air is what I appreciate about people. To go out and meet them you must go incredibly far.

DELICATELY FEELING

If the air is cold enough I feel something. It might only be on my arm or my hand, but it is there. All last year I wore a brooch pinned to my coat. I was conscious of it. When I walked down the street, I was lifted by the brooch. I was still walking on the ground, but some part of me was floating up, a small part of me.

These days it's colder and colder and I feel more. My skin is warm where my clothes touch me, and I sit in front of a heater like it's a fire. I bought a silk robe and it is the most beautiful thing I own. It's silver with faintly colorful flowers.

In the mornings my students lumber through the snow, trailing their bright mittens and hats, dropping them on the ground. I can see them coming a long way off, these different parts of them. In class I am bored and I talk and talk until my voice is its own separate thing. I don't know what children like. I have to watch cartoons or movies if I want to understand anything about them.

Last Saturday I saw a play about a war. Next to me sat a man and a woman. I had the feeling they wanted me to share the experience of the play with them. The woman's hair was braided and looped around her head. She looked expectantly at the stage, and sometimes at me. "Do you like this play?" she whispered. I whispered that though it was violent, I felt some affinity to it.

During intermission I went to the bathroom to reapply my lipstick and then I drank champagne in the lobby. The room was warm with people and I felt connected to them. I looked in their eyes and they looked back at me, sometimes for a long time.

Then the lights flickered, calling us back to the theater. Drunk from the sensations, I found my seat. This time the man was seated closest to me and he nodded at me as I sat down and he tried to hold my gaze. I nodded back, but didn't look at him for long because the play was starting and I didn't want to miss anything.

Now I felt an affinity so dearly to the actors that everything inside me was heartbreakingly connected. My experience of the moment heightened, but outside I remained calm.

Toward the end of the play the stage became chaotic, like fat horses were galloping over it. Men knocked each other down and struck each other in the faces and heads. Several women stood on the sidelines, screaming. I found myself getting angry at the screaming. "This is a play!" I yelled as loudly as I could. It was already so loud it didn't matter that I had yelled it. Then, when everyone was dead, including the women, the play was over. "Fuck you," I said, weakly. Everyone clapped. I started clapping too.

"Are you okay?" the man next to me asked.

"Yes."

"What's your name?" He asked me this question with more curiosity than I was expecting.

"Josephine."

"What a beautiful name. It's a pleasure to meet you, Josephine."

I put on my coat and gathered my things. The belt to my coat was tied very tightly around my waist.

"Yes, a pleasure," the woman said.

"You too." I kept tightening my belt. I didn't know if I should stay or leave, but finally made my way toward the doors. I turned around and the two of them were holding hands, watching me.

At the edge of a field, carrots grow in the dark soil. Green leaves mark them. A small animal moves in and out among the vegetables, eating. In my kitchen I prepare rice. I soak black beans. This is when we are most vulnerable; when we eat, when we prepare to.

When I was a child, I was nothing like my students. I wanted to see neon lights clustered near an ocean. In Shanghai, this came true. I walked along the Bundt and the air was like a thousand ovens. Late at night I lay in a bed "feeling the room." I must have been looking for something when I walked back and forth next to the water.

Though there are many ways in which I am the same now as I was then, I don't understand who I was as a child either.

In class, I ask the children to put on a play. Because they like the theater they are excited by this idea. One little girl is a trash truck. I tell her it would be better to play a person. She says she'll be a hobo. The children make fake snow out of cotton balls glued onto posterboard. They have so much fun building the set they are angry when they have to perform.

When they do perform, I get bored. There are seven of them "on stage" and two of them are reciting their Christmas lists. I pay attention as long as I can and then I stare at the blackboard and then at the clock.

"Are you watching!" the children shriek.

The bell rings and they drop everything, scattering into the hallway. Out in the street I cry because I know I am a bad teacher, but there is nothing else for me to do with my life. A huge pink doll sits in the window of a toy store in the middle of a miniature village, a train circling around her. I hate this scene.

I think about the couple. At night, when I read in my bed, or in the old armchair next to the window, it doesn't take long before the book is resting in my lap, closed, and I am aware of nothing but the inside of my mind. There the couple looks at me and I look at them.

When I pull carrots out of the soil, or snip chard from its pink stems, I imagine what their house must be like. I am sure there are drawings hanging on the walls and that a strong female dog guards them and keeps them safe. A dog they walk and let onto the couch on chilly evenings. If I want this kind of night it is mine.

When the weekend comes I go back to the theater. There, surrounded by other theatergoers, is my couple, just as I had imagined they would be. The woman gets up to meet me. She is wearing a dress made of a soft material. I let myself fall into her.

"Your skin is cold," she says.

"Too cold?"

"No."

The man takes my hand and holds it against his cheek. "I'm just going to come right out and ask. Are you married?"

"Not at all."

"That's terrific."

"Sit down," the woman says, motioning to the chair between them.

On stage is a man in a kitchen, putting groceries away. I sit there feeling the stage, feeling the whole theater. I can feel its history.

Because it is much quieter than the play before it we in the audience can hear each other breathe. The actor breathes too. He and I look at each other. Then he looks at the man next to me. The theater has turned into a living room.

"This is the front hallway. This is the bathroom. This is the bedroom." I say these things in a fragile voice.

The couple lingers at the door of my bedroom. "Would you like to go in?" I ask.

"Yes," the man answers.

They asked if they could visit me and now they are here. I freeze in front of my bed, a statue in my own rooms.

"We don't mean to frighten you," the woman says.

"I'm often frightened."

"Why?" the man asks.

"Life is frightening." I sigh. "But it is also tender."

"It is," the woman says. "And sometimes it becomes new."

"Should I change into something more comfortable?" I ask.

"Oh, yes," she says.

I take off my clothes, enjoying the feeling of being naked in front of the couple. I think they are finally scared. I pull the robe around me, closing it with its silk belt. Now nobody knows what to do. I kiss the woman and then I kiss the man. Then we stand there, terrified.

At school, I try to be present for my students. We make turkeys out of paper plates and construction paper, and after the children have drawn all over them in colors like pink and light green that are nothing like the colors of turkeys, they take off around the room, running with their new birds, sometimes slipping on them.

"Be careful, be careful," I yell.

On my walks I whisper to myself, "This couple, this couple, this couple."

"You're different than the others," the woman tells me.

"I'm different from myself," I say cheerfully, patting her hands with mine. The man is lying in my bed, waiting for me.

"Can I give you something?" she asks.

"I don't deserve anything."

"It doesn't matter."

She takes out a black velvet jewelry box. Inside the box is a delicate gold bracelet made for someone with much finer wrists than mine, someone with noble blood.

"It's pretty."

"Will you wear it?"

She puts the bracelet around my wrist and it shines in the lamp-light. The gold is both yellow and white.

"But what does it mean? Are you asking me to be in a relation-ship with you?"

The man comes out of the bedroom and stands in the hallway.

"Yes, we would like to stay with you forever."

I'm very warm now, especially around my wrist. I don't think I've ever been this warm before.

I wear the bracelet every day. I sleep with it, and I leave it on my wrist when I am taking a bath. I have told the couple that forever is a long time, and they don't seem to mind my lack of commitment.

"I am so much in the present," the woman says, "that it doesn't bother me to let go of the future."

"The future," I repeat dreamily. "I guess I wouldn't mind if it were an extension of this. It's just that I never imagined I would be in a long-term relationship with a married couple."

"We never thought of it either," the man says. He's wearing a wintery sweater. Everything is wintery now.

When I go to the grocery store I see the bracelet when I reach for things on the shelves. I see my whole arm. Even the children are drawn to its delicate nature, and one of them stares at it when he is supposed to be taking a spelling test. After the test is over the students go home and I stay behind to catch up on my grading. It is dark outside by the time I finish. The turkeys are stapled to a long bulletin board. When the heater kicks on I can hear the air come through the vents.

The school is over 100 years old. Time moves and the building stays still. The first students who went to this school are dead. I look at the turkeys and feel tender toward the children. The children like making things. They like the holidays.

At home, late, the woman calls.

"I just wanted to say good night."

"Are you going to sleep now?"

"Yes, I'm lying in bed. I'm thinking about you."

"I'm in my robe," I say. "I'm thinking about you too. Both of you."

"It's never just the two of us anymore," she says. "Whenever we're together you're here also."

I feel it, that I am there in that house; but I am here in this house too.

It's as if the couple has softened into one creature—what I am drawn to is singular. I move toward a relationship, not two. It's not the woman I crave, or the man. But, still, it's three bodies in a bed.

"Is this your life, Josephine?" I ask myself. "Are you here or are you there?"

But here or there is a tapestry of happiness and pain and joy and terror, so it doesn't really matter, a tapestry so large and colorful you can't see it all at once. It's hard to take in the number of lives imprinted upon it. If you get close you see one life and something of another, touching it.

The next time I go to the couple's house only the man is home, but as the woman has already proclaimed to me, she is present too, everywhere, even on the very tip of the man's shirtsleeve.

"Yes, yes," he agrees, "Gabby is with us."

In their dark bed I'm not even sure it's the man's body I'm touching or that is touching me, and when she comes home, hours later, her body doesn't feel so very different from his.

ACKNOWLEDGEMENTS

I wish to express my appreciation to the editors of the following publications, where some of these stories previously appeared: *Dear Navigator, Dewclaw, Joyland, Little Red Leaves, Moonlit,* and *Sidebrow*. "I Will Force This" was published as a Belladonna* chaplet under the title "Hunger," and "Tramps Everywhere" exists as a PARROT Series chapbook.

Passages in "Words Come to Me," "Queen," and "They've Been Bringing Them Here for Decades" are excerpted from Hannah Weiner's *Open House*, Clarice Lispector's *The Hour of the Star,* and Marguerite Duras' *Blue Eyes, Black Hair.*

With infinite thanks to Danielle Dutton and Martin Riker, and to Richard Yoo, Rachel Tredon, Alicia Scherson, Amarnath Ravva, Adam Novy, Nathanaël, Ravish Momin, Matthew Mazzotta, Todd Mattei, Laida Lertxundi, Angela Leonino, Taigen Dan Leighton, Jennifer Karmin, Matthew Goulish, Olivia Casanueva, Teresa Carmody, Alex Branch, Daniel Borzutzky, Brent Armendinger, and Amanda Ackerman, whose work, thinking, and friendship has inspired so much of this book.

ABOUT THE AUTHOR

Amina Cain is the author of *I Go to Some Hollow* (Les Figues Press, 2009). She lives and works in Los Angeles.

DOROTHY, A PUBLISHING PROJECT

1. Renee Gladman *Event Factory*
2. Barbara Comyns *Who Was Changed and Who Was Dead*
3. Renee Gladman *The Ravickians*
4. Manuela Draeger *In the Time of the Blue Ball*
5. Azareen Van der Vliet Oloomi *Fra Keeler*
6. Suzanne Scanlon *Promising Young Women*
7. Renee Gladman *Ana Patova Crosses a Bridge*
8. Amina Cain *Creature*

DOROTHYPROJECT.COM